TRUE'S BIRTHDAY PARTY

Adaptation from the animated series: Robin Bright

Illustrations: Guru Animation Studio Lt

CRACKBOOM!

It's True's birthday, and Bartleby has planned the most amazing party ever. True is so excited, she gives him a big hug. "You're the best, B!" she says.

All over the Rainbow Kingdom, preparations are underway. Yetis and Critters are gathering the decorations. Rainbow bus is bringing guests to True's birthday party.

But first Bartleby takes True on a birthday picnic.

"Ice cream for lunch! Can we do that?" asks True.

"Sure," says Bartleby, "It's your birthday!"

After lunch, Bartleby has another surprise for True.
"We're going to get you a new birthday suit!" After trying on several outfits, True settles on one that includes a cape and some gloves.
"This one is perfect!" says True.

In True's kitchen, Grizelda is baking a birthday cake...

It's strawnilla flavored,

with wiggly-jiggly jelly

and bubblechew icing.

When it comes to ingredients, "More is better!" claims Grizelda. "Princesses don't need recipes! We're amazing at everything we do."

But Grizelda puts too much
bubblechew icing into the pot.
There is so much of it, that the goo spills
onto the street and Rainbow Bus gets
stuck in it, causing a terrible traffic jam.
True's guests won't be able
to make it to the party!

Grizelda has also used too much wiggle-jiggle powder. Oh, no! The birthday cake wiggles and jiggles so hard that it causes an earthquake!

Trees all over the Neverending Forest begin to fall. "Time for some Wish help!" says True.

True calls Cumulo to take her and Bartleby to the Wishing Tree. Zee listens as True explains the situation. "That does sound serious," says Zee. "Let's sit and have a think."

True and Zee sit down on the mushrooms. They each take a deep breath. "First we need to help the trees get back upright in the Neverending Forest," True says. "Then we have to get the gooey glob off the streets of Rainbow City."

"The Wishing Tree has heard you, True," Zee says. "It's time to get your three Wishes."

WISHING TREE,
WISHING TREE,
PLEASE SHARE YOUR WONDERFUL
WISHES WITH ME.

The Wishes wake up and spin around True.
Three Wishes stay with her, and the others return
to the Wishing Tree.

"Very interesting Wishes," Zee says.
"I can tell you more about their powers.
Let's check the Wishopedia."

LIFTO
can lift anything you place on top of it.

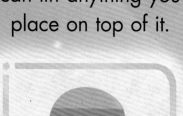

PUMPA
can blow air into anything.

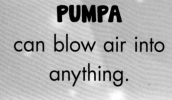

KAKARAKA
can break large objects into little pieces.

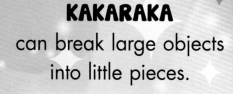

"Thank you, Zee. And thank you, Wishing Tree, for sharing your Wishes with me," True says, as she leaves with the Wishes in her pack.

Back in the Neverending Forest, True activates her first Wish. "Zip zap zoo, I choose you! Wake up, Lifto! Wish come true!" She places the Wish beneath a fallen tree.
Lifto pushes and lifts until the tree is standing up again!

ZIP ZAP ZOO!

"Come on, B," says True, "We have to get back to Rainbow City to deal with that gooey globby mess!"

When they get to Rainbow Bus, True activates her second Wish. She inserts Pumpa's nozzle into the gooey glob. "Pumpa power, go!" cries True. Pumpa begins to blow out air.

The glob inflates into a giant bubble that floats away. The road is clear!

"Thanks, Pumpa." says True. "That really blew me away!"

But there's more trouble with the cake.
It won't stop growing! "It's too big for the
oven, and the kitchen, and the house!"
cries Grizelda.

Suddenly, the giant cake pops out of True's house. It's magnificent! "A super huge birthday cake!" says True.

"Oh, B, you shouldn't have!" says True.

But the cake is so big, that it teeters, and topples over—right onto Mushroom Town!

"I'm trapped in a scrumptious strawnilla sponge cake!" cries the Rainbow King over facebubble. And so are the rest of True's birthday guests.

True calls Cumulo to bring her and Bartleby to Mushroom Town. "It's time for my third Wish," says True once they get there. She activates Kakaraka, who makes the cake explode. Luckily, the guests, decorations, and gifts all land safely back down.

Everyone is ready to celebrate True's birthday at last.
But now there's no birthday cake for True's party!

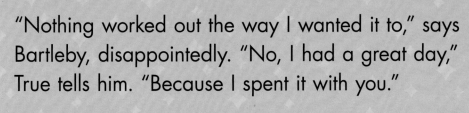

"Nothing worked out the way I wanted it to," says Bartleby, disappointedly. "No, I had a great day," True tells him. "Because I spent it with you."

But wait—pieces of strawnilla sponge cake are falling from the sky. "It's raining cupcakes!" True exclaims. "Happy birthday, True!" everyone shouts. "This is even better than the best party ever!" says True.

CrackBoom! Books is an imprint of Chouette Publishing (1987) Inc.

TRUE AND THE RAINBOW KINGDOM™/MC is a registered trademark of Guru Animation Studio Ltd.
All related characters, names and logos are trademarks of Guru Animation Studio Ltd. and its affiliated
companies.

Created by FriendsWithYou and produced by Guru Studio.

Story and illustrations used with permission of Guru Animation Studio Ltd. based on TRUE AND THE
RAINBOW KINGDOM™/MC episode 303: True's Birthday Party. © 2018 Guru True 3 Ltd.
All rights reserved. Original script written by Tom Berger, adapted by Robin Bright.

Chouette Publishing would like to thank the Government of Canada and SODEC
for their financial support.

Bibliothèque et Archives nationales du Québec and Library and Archives
Canada cataloguing in publication

Title: True's birthday party / adaptation, Robin Bright ; illustrations, Guru
Animation Studio.
Names: Bright, Robin, 1966- author. | Guru Studio (Firm), illustrator.
Description: Series statement: True and the rainbow kingdom
Identifiers: Canadiana 20210042176 | ISBN 9782898023088 (softcover)
Classification: LCC PZ7.1.B75 Tr 2021 | DDC j813/.6—dc23

Legal deposit – Bibliothèque et Archives nationales du Québec, 2021.
Legal deposit – Library and Archives Canada, 2021.

Printed in Dongguan, China
10 9 8 7 6 5 4 3 2 1   CHO2123 FEB2021
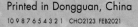